WITHDRAWN

To Simón and Leia, for turning my world upside down
and making every day an adventure.

A TEMPLAR BOOK

First published in the UK in 2017 by Templar Publishing,
an imprint of Kings Road Publishing, part of the Bonnier Publishing Group,
The Plaza, 535 King's Road, London, SW10 0SZ
www.bonnierpublishing.com

1 3 5 7 9 10 8 6 4 2

ISBN 978-1-78370-671-6

This book was typeset in Brandon Grotesque
The illustrations were created digitally and printed
in Pantone Warm Red and Pantone 300 (blue)

Designed by Genevieve Webster
Edited by Carly Blake

Printed in China

DINO

Diego Vaisberg

t

templar publishing

One day a gigantic egg
appeared in our backyard.

CRACK!

We thought it might be a giant canary . . .

TWEET!
TWEET!

. . . or one of those big lizards that show up
in the summer . . .

or maybe a huge tortoise.

But it wasn't any of those kinds of things.

It was a
dinosaur!

He was so cute and friendly
we decided to keep him.

We named him Dino
and from that day on
he was our pet.

Dino wasn't very big at first.

But he grew . . .

and grew . . .

and grew . . .

until soon . . .

He was **enormous!**

Having an enormous dinosaur in the house
can be **very** tricky.

SMASH!

So we let him play outside as much as possible.

Dino's favourite game is

"FETCH!"

. . . but he doesn't always manage to bring the ball back.

Making new friends at the park is
also quite a challenge. Dino's roaring for joy
can sometimes be misunderstood.

All the excitement of being outdoors
makes Dino very hungry . . .

and not just for food.

So we have to keep a close eye on him
if his tummy starts to rumble.

GURGLE!

Goldy is our pet too. Goldy is not food!

Neither is the postman!

Dino does make an excellent guard dog, though, because he is afraid of nothing.

Well, **almost** nothing!

If Dino gets upset there is always something
in his box of toys that will cheer him up
and keep him entertained until bath time.

"Time for bed, Dino."

Having an enormous dinosaur in the house
can be **very** tricky . . .

So imagine our surprise when
three more gigantic eggs
turned up in our backyard . . .

We had to get a **bigger** house!